NICK JR.

DORA the EXPLORER ®

Dora Helps Diego!

by Laura Driscoll
illustrated by Tom Mangano

Ready-to-Read

Simon Spotlight/Nick Jr.

New York   London   Toronto   Sydney

Based on the TV series *Dora the Explorer*® as seen on Nick Jr.®

SIMON SPOTLIGHT
An imprint of Simon & Schuster Children's Publishing Division
1230 Avenue of the Americas, New York, New York 10020
© 2007 Viacom International Inc. All rights reserved.
NICK JR., *Dora the Explorer*, and all related titles, logos, and characters are
registered trademarks of Viacom International Inc.

Manufactured in the United States of America
6 8 10 9 7

Library of Congress Cataloging-in-Publication Data
Driscoll, Laura.
Dora helps Diego! / by Laura Driscoll ; illustrated by Tom Mangano.
—1st ed.
p. cm. — (Dora the explorer) (Ready-to-read)
ISBN-13: 978-1-4169-1509-6 (pbk.)
ISBN-10: 1-4169-1509-5 (pbk.)
I. Mangano, Tom. II. Dora the explorer (Television program)
III. Title. IV. Series. V. Series: Ready-to-read.
PZ7.D79Dor 2007
2006009688

Hi! I am  .

DORA

 ,  , and I

DIEGO   BOOTS

need your help!

Oh, no!  is missing!

BABY JAGUAR

 cannot find him!

DIEGO

 and I

BOOTS

are helping find him.

DIEGO

Will you help too?

Great!

Help us find  !

BABY JAGUAR

Look up in that .

TREE

I see a .

TAIL

has a .

BABY JAGUAR TAIL

Does it belong to  ?

BABY JAGUAR

No.

It is a
SNAKE

getting out of the ☀.
SUN

Where is BABY JAGUAR ?

Look behind those .

FLOWERS

I see .

FEET

has .

BABY JAGUAR   FEET

Do they belong to  ?

BABY JAGUAR

No.

It is

ISA

working in her .

GARDEN

Where is ?

BABY JAGUAR

Look behind that trunk.

TREE

I see .

WHISKERS

 BABY JAGUAR has WHISKERS .

Do those WHISKERS belong

to BABY JAGUAR ?

No.

It is , that sneaky fox.

SWIPER

Where is  ?
BABY JAGUAR

Look behind the .

SLIDE

I see .

SPOTS

 has  .

BABY JAGUAR   SPOTS

Do they belong to  ?

BABY JAGUAR

No.

It is the scarf that

belongs to .
BENNY

Will we **ever** find  ?
BABY JAGUAR

We need to go back to

the Animal Rescue Center.

We open the  .

DOOR

We cannot believe it!

We see a  ,   ,
           TAIL   FEET

         , and   .
WHISKERS   SPOTS

Here is   !
           BABY JAGUAR

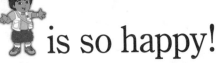 is so happy!

DIEGO

We found !

BABY JAGUAR

Thanks for helping!